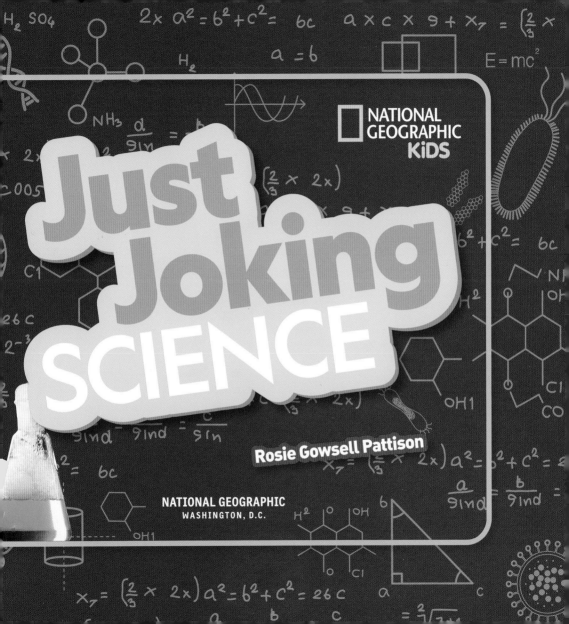

NATIONAL
GEOGRAPHIC
KiDS

Just Joking SCIENCE

Rosie Gowsell Pattison

NATIONAL GEOGRAPHIC
WASHINGTON, D.C.

Robot dogs can perform tasks like chasing a ball, sitting on command, or even taking themselves to a charging station!

4

Q What kind of scientist do you become after eating too many beans?

A A gas-tronomer.

Say this fast three times:

A physicist insists she lists her visits.

Q Why did the robot hire a tutor?

A Because his skills were getting rusty.

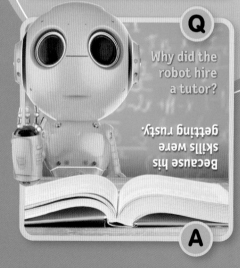

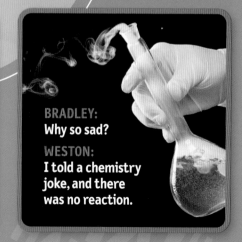

BRADLEY: Why so sad?

WESTON: I told a chemistry joke, and there was no reaction.

KNOCK, KNOCK.

Who's there?
Atom.
Atom who?
Up and atom, it's time to leave!

Atoms are tiny particles that are the building blocks of all matter. Even this raven is made up of atoms!

KNOCK, KNOCK.

Who's there?
Argon.
Argon who?
I miss you when you argon.

Argon is a colorless, odorless gas that is found in the atmosphere and in Earth's crust.

8

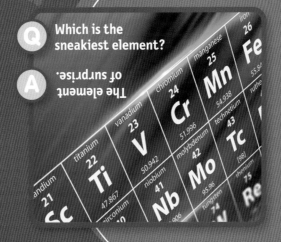

Q Which is the sneakiest element?

A The element of surprise.

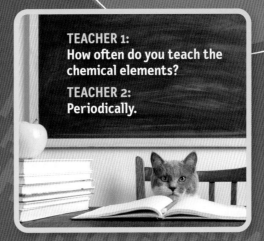

TEACHER 1:
How often do you teach the chemical elements?

TEACHER 2:
Periodically.

Q How do plants greet each other?

A They in-tree-duce themselves.

Q Why is a thermometer so smart?

A Because it has many degrees.

SYLVIA: Do you like the way Earth rotates?

MALIA: Oh, yes, it really makes my day.

Q What kind of scientist is handy if you have a leaky roof?

A A pail-eontologist.

Neon comes in both liquid and gas form. It is often used to make light-up signs because, under certain conditions, it glows a reddish orange color.

11

LABORATORY LAUGHS

RESEARCH: Penguin Poop Project

What to do with penguin poop? Well, if you're a NASA scientist, you might study it from space!

No, really. To help study climate change, space scientists want to know what Adélie penguins are eating. Here's the deal: Adélie penguins love eating shrimplike krill (which are reddish orange). If penguins are eating only krill , their poop will be orange. If they are eating mostly silverfish (which are blue), their poop will be blue. And it turns out scientists get the best view of this colorful poop from space.

So how does intergalactic poop patrol tell space scientists what's going on with the climate here on Earth, you ask? Good question! More blue poop means penguins are eating more silverfish than krill. A change in diet for these penguins is an indicator of how the food chain is changing. Less krill availability could mean populations are declining due to over-fishing and rapidly warming climates. Tracking changes in ecosystems is complicated, but space poop photos give scientists large-scale data on how things are going back here on Earth. So, keep up the good work, penguins and scientists!

Adélie penguins can dive as deep as 575 feet (175 m) in search of fish.

Adélie penguin parents will make their babies chase them before vomiting up krill for the chicks to eat.

SCIENCE
SILLINESS

14

I THINK I OVERDID IT ON THE SUNSCREEN.

NAME **Professor Hermit**

FIELD OF STUDY
Artifi-shell intelligence

FAVORITE PASTIME
Crabbing a burger with friends

PET PEEVE
Tan lines

Q Which **scientist** always **stays calm?**

A A serene biologist.

Q **What kind of scientist knows the most about barbecues?**

A A meat-eorologist.

Terrible science fair ideas:

- Why Does My Belly Button Smell?

- Guess What Number I'm Thinking Of

- Rocks Are Heavy and Other Obvious Observations

- Germs and Where to Find Them

- Gatorade Does Not Actually Help Alligators

Q What kind of android should you bring on a boat?

A A row-bot.

COOPER:
Are you going to finish that atom?

LEAH:
Why, do you want to split it?

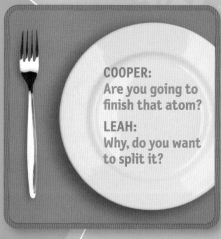

Q Why did the archaeologist laugh while digging up old bones?

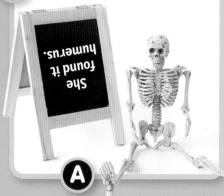

A She found it humerus.

Q Why should you never trust an atom?

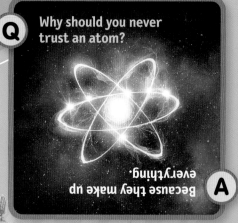

A Because they make up everything.

KNOCK, KNOCK.

Who's there?
Interrupting robot.
Interrupting ro—
BEEP BOOP BOP.

Aibo the robot dog has been programmed to recognize people's faces.

19

A hertz is a unit of measurement. It measures how many times something repeats in one second.

Q What do chemists' dogs do with their bones?

A They barium!

GARY: What are you reading?
CATHIE: A book on antigravity.
GARY: Is it good?
CATHIE: I can't put it down!

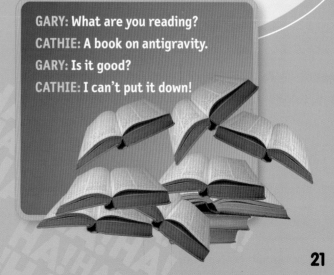

A watt is a way of measuring the rate that electrical energy is flowing.

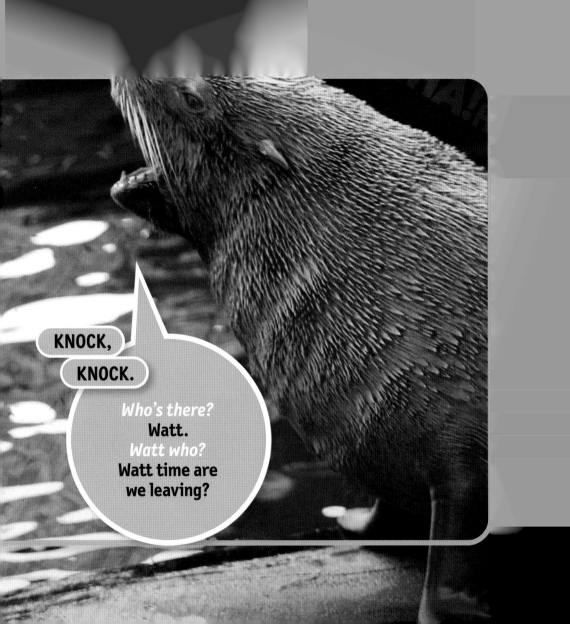

Say this fast three times:

A botanist's wish list.

Q

What do scientists decorate at Christmastime?

A A chemis-tree.

Q

Where do you put a nucleus that breaks the law?

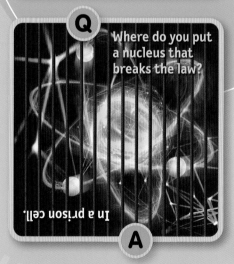

In a prison cell.

A

Why are protons so much fun to be around? **Q**

Because they are always so positive. **A**

24

Quick question: Cow-come cattle congregate in a common direction? Because they have animal magnetism! It's no joke: Cattle actually do face the same direction while grazing outdoors. It's a scientific fact.

For a long time, people believed cows acted this way to protect themselves from predators. Like all herd animals, cows stick together to survive. But why face in just one direction? Wouldn't it make more sense to have "guard cows" facing all directions? So, scientists turned to good old-fashioned scientific research. It showed that cattle have internal compasses that make them line up in a north-south direction.

Scientists studied satellite images of cattle across six continents and found that whatever the breed or the time, cattle oriented themselves north-south. Scientists don't yet know the significance of the magnetic alignment. But they do know that other animals such as birds, turtles, and some fish also use Earth's magnetic field—to guide their migrations. Scientists think humans may have magnetic compasses as well, which would make us closer to our cow cousins than we ever thought!

A cow's main stomach can hold up to 50 gallons (189 L) of partially digested food.

There are four different compartments in a cow's stomach.

Cattle drink about a bathtub full of water every day.

26

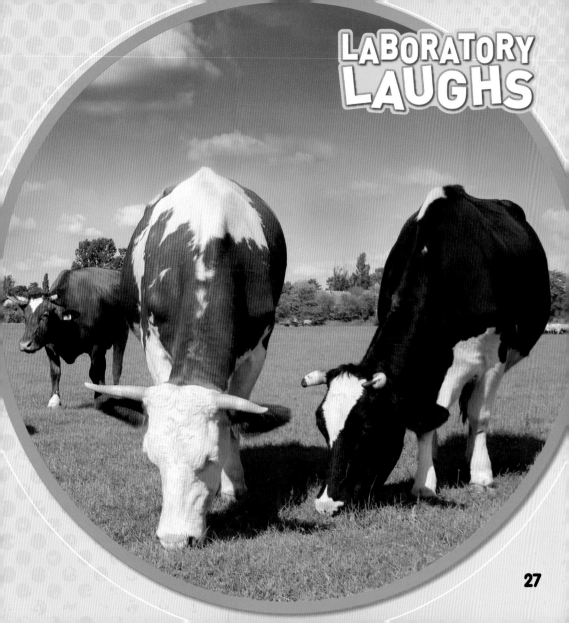

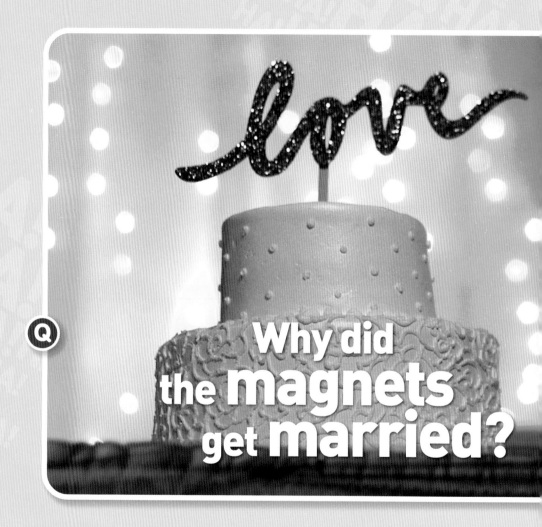

Q Why did the magnets get married?

Because they found each other attractive.

(A)

29

... AND DON'T GET DIRTY! WE ARE GOING OUT THIS AFTERNOON!
UH-OH.
SCIENCE SILLINESS

NAME **Puddles**

FAVORITE ACTIVITY
Testing water quality

REASON FOR STUDYING WATER
A thirst for knowledge

FAVORITE SAYING
Let's H$_2$Go!

31

Q What does an astronaut do after docking her spaceship?

A Put money in the parking meteor.

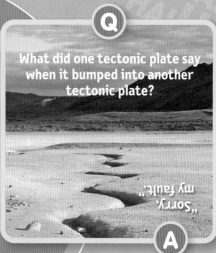

Q What did one tectonic plate say when it bumped into another tectonic plate?

A "Sorry, my fault."

Q Why can't you take **electricity** to a **party?**

A Because it doesn't know how to conduct itself.

MARIE: I've started a gardening business.

FRASER: Are you making lots of money?

MARIE: I'm raking it in!

To breathe, a fish gulps water into its mouth and filters it through the hairlike bristles in its gills. The oxygen is absorbed and the water is pushed out.

KNOCK, KNOCK.

Who's there?
Annie.
Annie who?
Annie one know the answers to the science quiz?

Q What's black and white, gives milk, and orbits Earth?

A The mooooon.

Q Why did the robot cross the road?

A Because it was programmed to do it.

34

Fission is the process of splitting an atom in two. This releases a lot of energy that can be used to create electricity.

KNOCK, KNOCK.

Who's there?
Fission.
Fission who?
Want to go fission on Saturday?

35

LABORATORY LAUGHS

Science has given us many important and life-changing discoveries over the years. This is not one of those experiments.

If you try to break a single, uncooked spaghetti noodle in half, you will end up with noodle shards everywhere. It is seemingly impossible to break a spaghetti noodle (known in scientific terms as a "brittle rod") in two pieces. When an uncooked noodle is bent in half, it first snaps in two, but then those broken pieces begin to flex backward, creating waves that break the spaghetti into even more pieces. This happens faster than the human eye can see.

So, is it possible to stop this from happening? It is! But you will need a specially built machine and a bunch of scientists from the Massachusetts Institute of Technology to make it happen. These scientists built a noodle bending machine and used it to flex and torque thousands of noodles. They found the perfect combination of bends and twists that need to be applied to the noodle—er, brittle rod—to counteract the flexing, and voilà! The perfect break! Just two pieces of broken noodle! Easy peasy (if you have a specially built machine, thousands of noodles, a world-class scientist, and a lot of time on your hands)!

The exact two-piece-breakage formula is: twist 270 degrees and bend the ends at 3 millimeters a second.

Nobel Prize-winning physicist Richard Feynman was known to have studied "spaghetti physics."

Scientists have also studied why coffee spills while walking with a full mug.

Q What is a chemist's favorite type of dog?

A A Laboratory retriever.

Q What do planets like to read?

A Comet books.

Acid is a type of chemical that can be very dangerous but also very helpful. We have acid in our stomachs to digest our food.

39

STAR:
Can I make you something to eat?

MOON:
No thanks, I'm full.

Q

What kind of **tree** can fit in a **botanist's** hand?

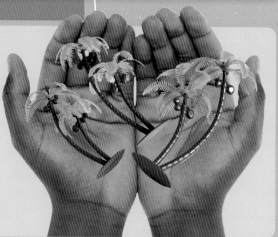

A palm tree.

A

Not-so-scientific discoveries:

- There are more human feet in the world than people.
- Being awake is the number one cause of sleeplessness.
- People who have more birthdays live longer.
- A minute passes every 60 seconds.
- Chickens don't have fingers.

Climate measures the
weather conditions of
one area over 30 years
or more. It tracks
humidity, temperature,
rain, snow, and wind.

Q Why are **chemists** **so good at** **solving problems?**

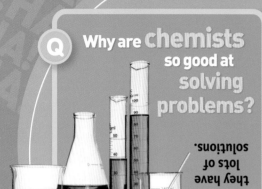

A Because they have lots of solutions.

Say this fast three times:

Professor Whistle threw three thistles.

Q What do scientists use to freshen their breath?

A Expert-mints.

Q Why can't you **trust** a **mathematician** holding **graph paper?**

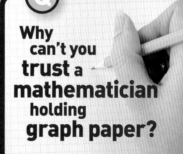

A Because she must be plotting something.

KNOCK, KNOCK.

Who's there?
Ion.
Ion who?
My mom told me to keep an ion my little brother.

An ion is an atom with a positive or negative electrical charge.

45

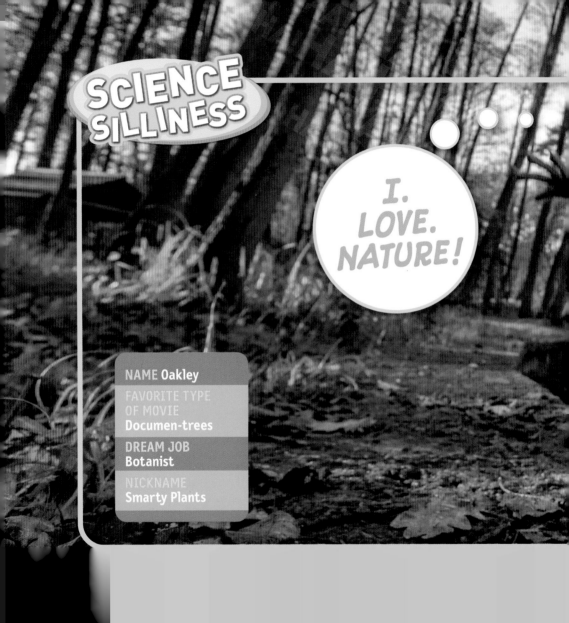

SCIENCE SILLINESS

I. LOVE. NATURE!

NAME **Oakley**

FAVORITE TYPE OF MOVIE
Documen-trees

DREAM JOB
Botanist

NICKNAME
Smarty Plants

KYLIE:
Are you enjoying chemistry class?

JORJA:
Oh yes, I'm really in my element!

Q

What did the second place winner in the astronomy contest win?

A

A constellation prize.

KNOCK, KNOCK.

Who's there?
Surgeon.
Surgeon who?
Surgeon for my cat. Have you seen her?

Surgeons and nurses wear special clothing in an operating room to make sure that they are germ free.

LABORATORY LAUGHS

Ever wonder what pigeons hang on the walls of their nests? Well, if it's artwork, these birds have a critical eye. That's right, those pesky birds hanging around the park are now art critics, and their beady eyes are not always kind.

A researcher in Tokyo taught pigeons to judge the artwork of children aged 9 to 11 so he could determine if a bird brain could understand "the human concept of beauty." Turns out, they could! First, the researchers showed the birds examples of "good" and "bad" artwork. The pigeons were rewarded with a treat when they pecked at the "good" pictures. They were trained to do nothing if shown a "bad" drawing.

Then, the eagle-eyed art critics were shown a number of paintings done by professional and, um, *fledgling* artists. The same works of art were judged by a panel of 10 human judges. The feathered and human judges agreed: The newbies' art was fowl. This showed that birds could measure "good" from "bad" in color and pattern, and place it in a pecking order.

Pigeons are highly intelligent and can also recognize themselves in a mirror.

The birds had no reaction to monochromatic, or black-and-white, paintings, likely meaning they used color to help make their judgments.

Some pigeons were trained to tell pastel paintings from watercolors.

SCIENCE SILLINESS

I'M TESTING HOW AERODYNAMIC I AM!

NAME **Harry**

FAVORITE SAYING
"I'm pretty fly."

FAVORITE FOOD
Plane pizza

DREAM JOB
Aerospace engineer

Q What do you do with a claustrophobic astronomer?

A Give him a little space.

Q Why are bacteria so fancy?

A Because they're very cultured.

Q Where do **marine biologists** go on **vacation?**

A Finland.

Q What kind of scientist can jump higher than a building?

A Any kind—buildings can't jump.

55

Q
What's a gorilla's favorite month?

A Ape-ril.

SCIENTIST: What do we want?!
CHEERING CROWD: Time travel!
SCIENTIST: When do we want it?
CHEERING CROWD: Last week!

What do space turkeys say?

"Hubble, hubble."

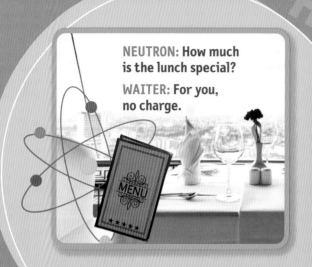

NEUTRON: How much is the lunch special?

WAITER: For you, no charge.

Q How can you tell when bees are happy?

A They hum while they work.

Hedgehogs will sometimes chew up poisonous plants and then spread the plant-saliva mixture on their spines. This gives them extra protection against predators.

KNOCK, KNOCK.

Who's there?
Y-axis.
Y-axis who?
Y-axis to come over if you won't let us in?

61

Q What kind of **pictures** do **microbiologists** take?

A Cell-fies.

Q What do you call an educated tube?

A A graduated cylinder.

Q How do you know when the moon is running out of money?

A When it's down to its last quarter.

Q What do plants have when they are a little bit hungry?

A A light snack.

NAME **Dr. McCavity**

FAVORITE COUNTRY
Brussia

FAVORITE ANIMAL
Molar bear

FAVORITE TYPE OF BOAT
The tooth ferry

Q

Why are moon dogs so itchy?

A Because they have lunar-ticks.

Q What kind of music do planets listen to?

A Nep-tunes.

66

Around 60 percent of the human body is made up of water.

KNOCK, KNOCK.

Who's there?
Water.
Water who?
Water you doing in my house?!

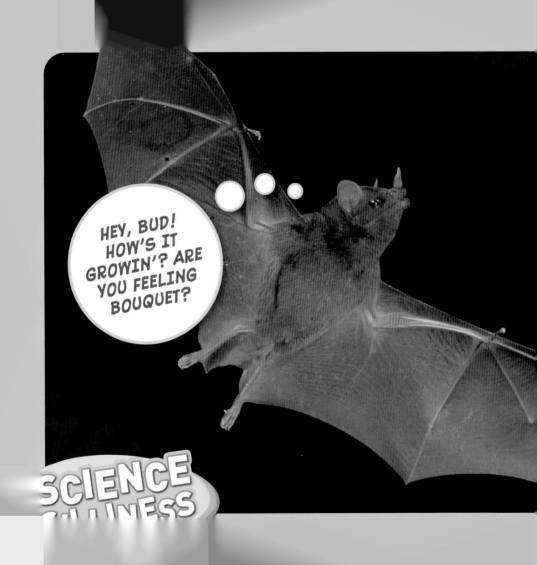

NAME **Dr. Jasmine**

SCHOOL ATTENDED
Flora-da Universi-tree

FAVORITE SAYING
"Get clover it!"

PET PEEVE
People who bud in

Q When are astronauts hungry?

A At launch-time.

Q What do **biologists** wear when they are **going out?**

A Designer genes.

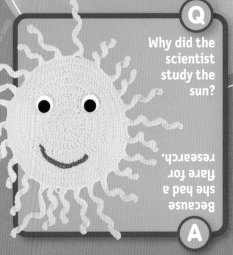

Q Why did the scientist study the sun?

A Because she had a flare for research.

Q Why do **mathematicians** make great **dancers?**

A Because they have good algorithm.

Elephants spend 12 to 18 hours every day eating plants, grass, and fruit. That's some serious snacking!

KNOCK, KNOCK.

Who's there?
Anita.
Anita who?
Anita microscope. Can I borrow yours?

RESEARCH: Tired Tortoises?

Everybody knows that yawning is contagious. The mere mention of a yawn can make you want to open your yap and breathe in deep. You're probably doing it right now, aren't you? You can likely make your friends or family yawn, too. But what about a turtle?

That's the question scientist Dr. Anna Wilkinson asked. And answered. Dr. Wilkinson wrote a paper on her research entitled "No Evidence of Contagious Yawning in The Red-Footed Tortoise."

Dr. Wilkinson spent more than six months trying to teach a red-footed tortoise to yawn on command. The teaching involved a lot of "stimulus" work, during which Dr. Wilkinson and her team rewarded the turtle every time it opened her mouth when the stimulus (a small square of paper) was presented. Once the tortoise learned to respond, it was introduced to others of its kind to see if the yawning could be made contagious. It could not. The research may seem dull, but Dr. Wilkinson says it shows that contagious yawning may require the ability to understand and share the feelings of others. Otherwise known as empathy, that ability is more likely to occur in social animals like dogs and primates.

The average length of a yawn is six seconds.

Red-footed tortoises can live more than 50 years.

Dr. Wilkinson earned an Ig Nobel Prize—that's a prize awarded by real Nobel Prize winners to fellow scientists whose research makes them laugh— and then think!

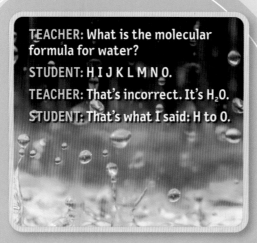

TEACHER: What is the molecular formula for water?

STUDENT: H I J K L M N O.

TEACHER: That's incorrect. It's H₂O.

STUDENT: That's what I said: H to O.

Q What do chickens grow in the garden?

A Eggplants.

74

Zinc is a type of metal. It can be found in minerals, ocean water, and even in our bodies!

KNOCK, KNOCK.

Who's there?
Zinc.
Zinc who?
Zinc you can open zee door?

75

SCIENCE SILLINESS

NAME Captain Ted

FAVORITE FOOD
Fish and ships

FAVORITE PASTIME
Taking the sea-nic route

PET PEEVE
Stern people

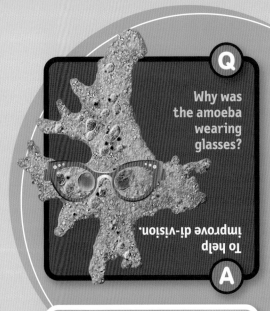

Q Why was the amoeba wearing glasses?

A To help improve di-vision.

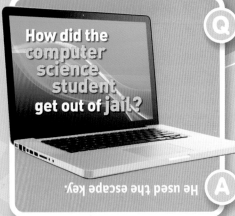

Q How did the computer science student get out of jail?

A He used the escape key.

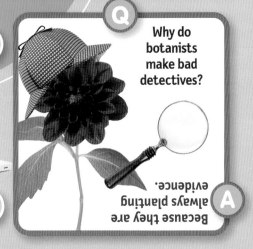

Q Why do botanists make bad detectives?

A Because they are always planting evidence.

78

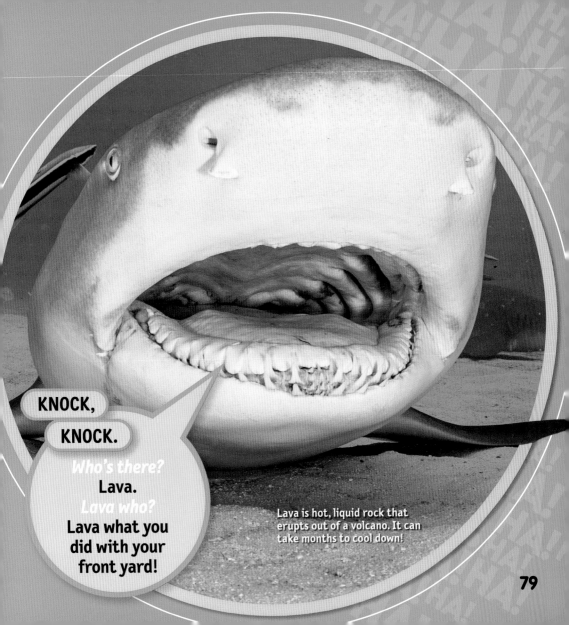

KNOCK, KNOCK.

Who's there?
Lava.
Lava who?
Lava what you did with your front yard!

Lava is hot, liquid rock that erupts out of a volcano. It can take months to cool down!

79

Q What do you call a **cashew** on a **spaceship?**

A An astro-nut.

Q Why couldn't the **flower** ride its **bike?**

A Because it lost its petals.

Science fair slogans:

- Geology Rocks!
- Geography Is Where It's At
- Seismology: It's Not Your Fault
- Biology—It Grows on You!
- Entomology: What's Bugging You?

SOLAR ENERGY

WHY DOGS ARE BETTER THAN CATS

KNOCK, KNOCK.

Who's there?
Amoeba.
Amoeba who?
Amoeba wrong, but have we met before?

Amoebas are one-celled organisms shaped like blobs. They can only be seen under a microscope.

Q

What did the
big flower
say to the
little flower?

A "What's up, bud?"

Q What did the **botanist** get when she took a **tree** into a **sauna?**

A Sweaty palms.

83

Q

Why are plants great cheerleaders?

GO SEEDS!

Because they are always rooting for you.

KNOCK, KNOCK.

Who's there?
Iva.
Iva who?
Iva lot of science experiments to do.

A flamingo's beak is lined with hairy fibers that filter mud and dirt from the food the bird scoops out of the water. This process happens while the flamingo's head is upside down!

Famous botanists:

- Miley Iris
- Elvis Parsley
- Justin Leaver
- Spruce Springsteen
- Lily Eilish
- Maroon Chive

METEOR 1: How was your shower?

METEOR 2: It was out of this world!

Q Why don't you ever see botanists hiding in trees?

A Because they are good at it.

Q How did the oceanographer cut the tide in half?

A With a sea-saw.

Q Why aren't marine biologists funny?

A Because their jokes are wearing fin.

Q Why did the cloud like being with the fog?

A Because it was so down-to-earth.

Gas is a state of matter, along with liquids and solids. Gases are usually invisible.

KNOCK, KNOCK.

Who's there?
Gas.
Gas who?
I told you to gas!

89

Q Why did the
germ
cross the
microscope?

A To get to the other slide.

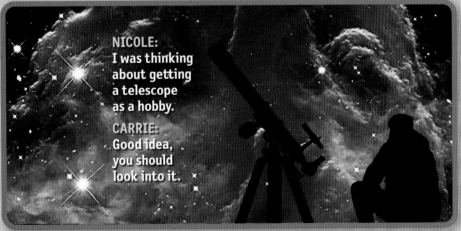

NICOLE:
I was thinking about getting a telescope as a hobby.

CARRIE:
Good idea, you should look into it.

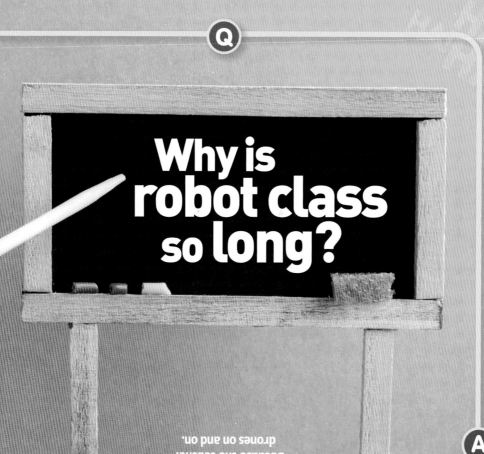

Q

Why is robot class so long?

A

Because the teacher drones on and on.

LABORATORY LAUGHS

Can You Swim in Syrup?

Slow as molasses! If you're a poky walker who likes to amble down the street to your own beat, you may have heard this comparison from, say, a frustrated parent or grandparent. But have you ever thought about whether walking in molasses would really make you sluggish? What about syrup? Would that slow you down?

Lucky for you, science has answered that question! And the answer is no. Researchers at the University of Minnesota actually conducted an experiment that had a team of elite and average swimmers stroking through guar gum to see if it was as easy as water. Guar gum is an edible thickener used in some ice cream and salad dressings. A ton of it (more or less) was dumped into a swimming pool for the test. Beyond the creepy sensation that they were swimming in snot, the test subjects reported no real difference. Their stroke times were not much different either.

Researchers concluded that for humans, swimming speed depends more on thrust and power than on the gloopy matter they propel through.

Swimming uses almost every muscle in the human body.

Swimmers sweat in the pool as much as other athletes sweat on land.

Some competitive swimmers shave their hair to reduce drag in the water.

Say this fast three times:

Seething sea season.

Q Where do geologists put their dirty dishes?

A In the zinc.

Q What is the **dullest** element?

A Borium.

Q What did silver say to gold when he saw it skipping school?

A "Au, U! Get to class!"

Saturn is the second biggest planet in our solar system. It rotates very quickly—one day on Saturn is only 10 hours and 14 minutes long!

KNOCK, KNOCK.

Who's there?
Saturn.
Saturn who?
Saturn that frown upside down!

What did the zoologist say to the swordfish?

Q

"Lookin' sharp!" **A**

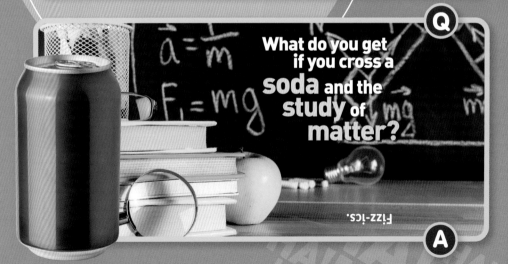

Q

What do you get if you cross a **soda** and the **study** of **matter?**

Fizz-ics. **A**

KNOCK,
KNOCK.

Who's there?
T. rex.
T. rex who?
There's a T. rex at your door and you want to know its name?!

A T. rex had around 60 teeth that were each about the size of a banana.

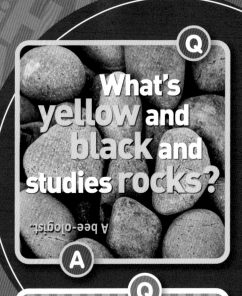

Q

What's yellow and black and studies rocks?

A A bee-ologist.

Q

Where do astronauts catch up with friends?

A On Spacebook.

Q

What's a physicist's favorite food?

A Fission chips.

Q

Where does light go when it breaks the law?

A To prism.

Thistles have sharp thorns to prevent them from being eaten by grazing animals.

KNOCK, KNOCK.

Who's there?
Thistle.
Thistle who?
Thistle have to wait until after dinner.

103

Why couldn't the **astronaut** book a **room** on the **moon?**

Because it was full.

OCEANOGRAPHER 1:
Did you read my report on oceans?

OCEANOGRAPHER 2:
Yes, but it needs more information.

OCEANOGRAPHER 1:
Should I be more Pacific?

Q

How does the sun listen to music?

A

On the ray-dio.

106

An orca's body is covered in a fatty tissue called blubber. Blubber keeps an orca's body warm and is broken down to provide energy when food is scarce.

KNOCK, KNOCK.

Who's there?
Unit.
Unit who?
Unit these mittens? They are nice!

Q What is an astronomer's favorite button on a keyboard?

A The space bar.

Q Why did the zoologist buy a chick?

A Because it was cheep.

108

Q What did one grumpy botanist say to another?

A "Leaf me alone."

Say this fast three times:

Rudder valve reversals.

Q Why did the scientist remove his doorbell?

A He wanted to win the No-bell Prize.

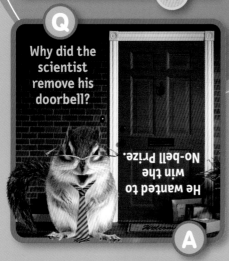

Q What do mathematicians find odd?

A Numbers not divisible by two.

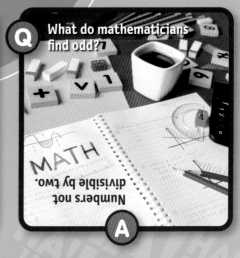

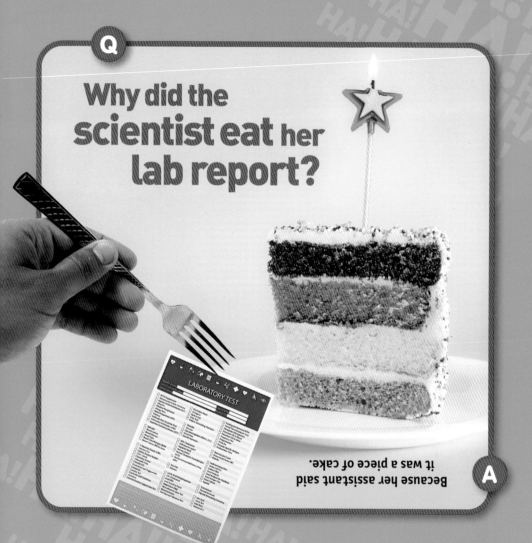

Q

Why did the scientist eat her lab report?

A

Because her assistant said it was a piece of cake.

111

IN THIS DISGUISE I CAN CONTINUE MY SHARK STUDIES UNNOTICED!

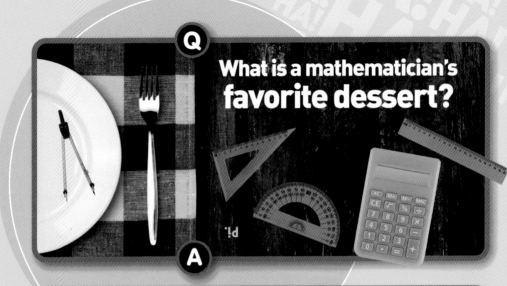

Q

What is a mathematician's favorite dessert?

A pi.

Q

Why did the **obtuse triangle fail** its test?

A Because it was never right.

115

RESEARCH: It's Still Good ... Right?

You dropped your cookie on the floor. No worries, you can still pick it up, dust it off, and down it. Or can you? As rumor goes, if you pull it off the floor within five seconds of impact, you're okay to eat it. But is there any science behind that?

And the answer is: no, nope, nada. Scientists at Rutgers University worked long and hard on this one. Many cookies were sacrificed in the name of research. Actually, they used watermelon, gummy candy, plain bread, and, just to make it gross and messy, buttered bread. They also used four test surfaces: stainless steel, tile, wood, and carpet. They even upped the numbers by testing for a five second, 30 second, and 300 second "on floor" time. After spreading millions of bacteria on the testing surfaces, they dropped the food.

What the researchers found is that no matter what, the food picked up bacteria. The longer it sat, the more bacteria it picked up. Juicy watermelon and buttery bread picked up the most. Surprisingly, the carpet surface transferred fewer bacteria. Debunking the five-second rule might not prevent people from scarfing dropped food, but with science to the rescue, at least we know the risks.

There are "good" bacteria that live in our bodies. They are mainly used in digestion.

Bacteria can reproduce once every 20 minutes.

Some bacteria can generate light. This is called bioluminescence.

NAME Sneezy

CAUSE OF ILLNESS
Bark-teria

SYMPTOMS
**Feeling melan-collie,
husky voice**

DIAGNOSIS
**You'll be pup and running
in no time!**

Q What's small, red, and whispers in the garden?

PSST PSST

A A hoarse-radish.

METEOROLOGIST 1: Looks like we have a lot of rain coming our way. Wouldn't you agree?

METEOROLOGIST 2: Oh, without a drought.

Q Which planet is the fanciest?

A Saturn, because it wears a lot of rings.

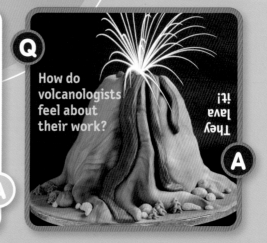

Q How do volcanologists feel about their work?

A They lava it!

120

There are around 500,000 earthquakes recorded every year.

KNOCK, KNOCK.

Who's there?
Quake.
Quake who?
Quake up, sleepyhead!

121

Q What is a meteorologist's favorite party game?

A Twister.

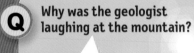

Q Why didn't the gardener plant any flowers?

A She hadn't botany!

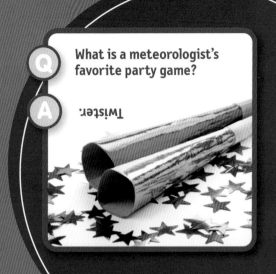

Q Why was the geologist laughing at the mountain?

A Because she thought it was hill-arious.

TEACHER: We only have half a day of school this morning.

STUDENTS: Hooray!

TEACHER: We'll have the other half this afternoon.

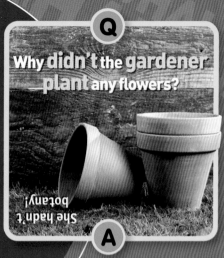

122

KNOCK, KNOCK.

Who's there?
Nobel.
Nobel who?
There's Nobel so I knocked.

The Nobel Prize is one of the most respected awards in the world. Many famous scientists have won for their important discoveries or research.

What do astronauts snack on?

Rocket chips.

BEN:
Did you hear the comedian's joke about earthquakes?

MAIRI:
I did. It really cracked me up!

Q What did the botanist get when she crossed poison ivy and a four-leaf clover?

A A rash of good luck.

126

An electric eel can release an electrical charge five times more powerful than a wall socket in your house!

KNOCK, KNOCK.

Who's there?
Alec.
Alec who?
Did your Alec-tricity go out?

127

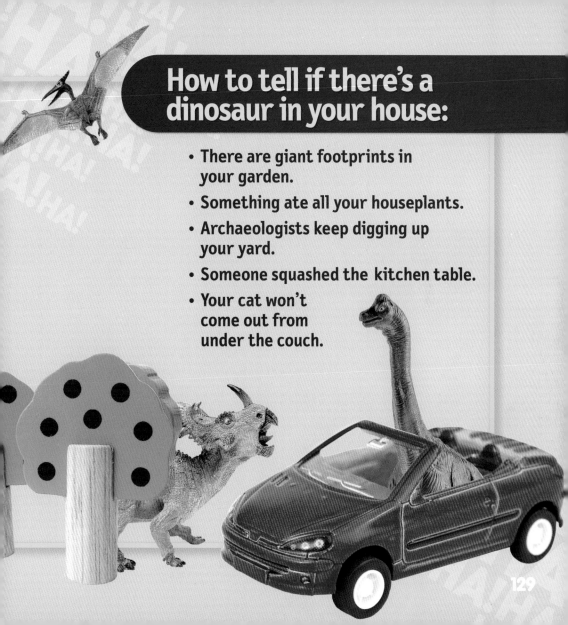

How to tell if there's a dinosaur in your house:

- There are giant footprints in your garden.
- Something ate all your houseplants.
- Archaeologists keep digging up your yard.
- Someone squashed the kitchen table.
- Your cat won't come out from under the couch.

ZOOLOGIST 1:
I left the gate open, and a bunch of animals wandered into the parking lot!

ZOOLOGIST 2:
Uh-oh! We're going to have a huge giraffe-ic jam out there!

Q What is a **meteorologist's** favorite animal?

A Rain-deer.

A hippopotamus produces its own sunblock! It sweats an oily red liquid that keeps its skin from drying out and protects it from the sun.

KNOCK, KNOCK.

Who's there?
Alex.
Alex who?
Alex-plain our science homework to you.

131

Q Where do geologists like to sit?

A In rocking chairs.

Say this fast three times:

Omnivorous octopus.

Q Why isn't there a clock in the science lab?

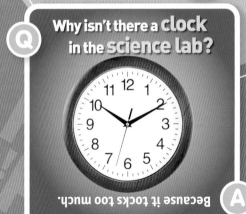

A Because it tocks too much.

Q What did one DNA strand say to another DNA strand?

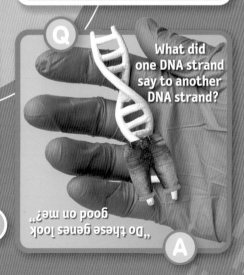

A "Do these genes look good on me?"

KNOCK, KNOCK.

Who's there?
Liter.
Liter who?
There's garbage everywhere out here! Who's the liter-bug?

A liter is a unit of measurement used mainly for liquids.

SCIENCE SILLINESS

NAME Flash

FAVORITE TYPE OF BOOK
Cat-alogs

FAVORITE PASTIME
Bird spotting (and eating!)

AREA OF STUDY
Hiss-tory

Q

Who did Dr. Frankenstein bring to the prom?

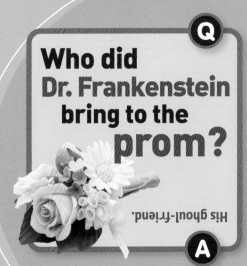

A His ghoul-friend.

Q

What did the diamond say to the pyrite?

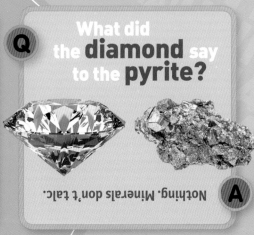

A Nothing. Minerals don't talc.

Q Why did the oceanographer never learn the alphabet?

A Because she got lost at C.

Q How do you catch a runaway computer scientist?

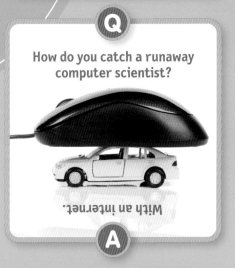

A With an internet.

A laser produces a powerful beam of light. This light can do many things like cut through objects or carry internet signals long distances.

KNOCK, KNOCK.

Who's there?
Laser.
Laser who?
Time to go. It's laser than you think!

137

LABORATORY LAUGHS

RESEARCH: A Man in Bear's Clothing

File this under "scientist makes the most out of Halloween costume." In Norway, where scientists take their wildlife research seriously, a team of crack investigators wanted to know if climate change was making reindeer less fearful of polar bears. Polar bears are top predators that normally spend most of their time away from land hunting for seals on polar ice floes. But a warming polar climate means they are spending more time on land in reindeer territory. This means reindeer might be getting used to the bears and, as a result, losing some of their protective wary behavior.

The researchers could not use a real bear to test their ideas. Lacking a costume store on their tundra research site, they did what every last-minute Halloween dress-up fan does—they improvised! Using white clothing and a white thermal face mask, the scientist dressed as a "bear" then approached groups of reindeer. Measuring the distance at which the reindeer showed fear and flight, the scientists concluded that they showed fear sooner with the bear costume than with humans dressed in regular clothing alone.

The researchers say they aren't done with their dress-up just yet. Next time, they hope to measure their results after using a better bear costume.

Both male and female reindeer have antlers. In other species of deer, only the male has them.

During one part of the experiment, researchers were interrupted by a real polar bear approaching the group of reindeer they were studying.

Reindeer have fur on the bottom of their hooves to keep from slipping on icy surfaces.

139

Q Why did the **chemistry professor** put on **sunglasses?**

A Because her students were so bright.

Q What kind of flowers grow on the stars?

A Sunflowers.

Q Why did the zoologist study a baguette in a cage?

A Because it was bread in captivity.

Q Who is in charge of the lightning orchestra?

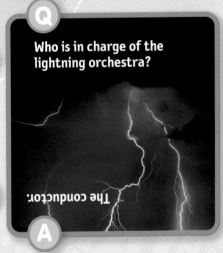

A The conductor.

143

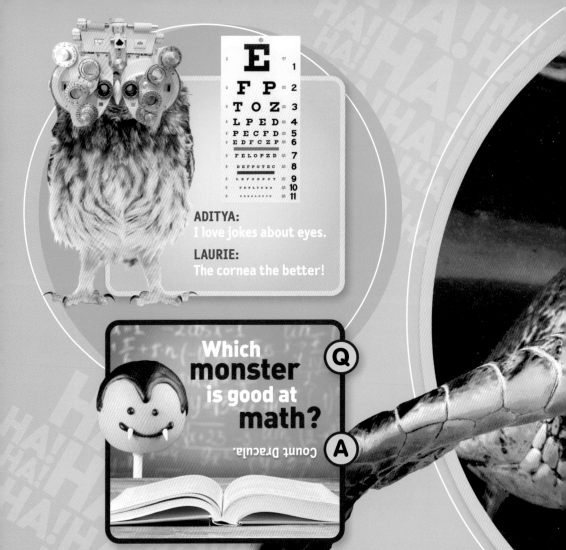

ADITYA:
I love jokes about eyes.

LAURIE:
The cornea the better!

Q Which **monster** is good at **math?**

A Count Dracula.

144

KNOCK, KNOCK.

Who's there?
Gram.
Gram who?
I gram getting tired of knocking.

Warmer sand temperatures around a **sea turtle's nest** will produce more female **hatchlings.** Cooler temperatures lead to more male baby turtles.

145

OCK,
KNOCK.

Who's there?
Atomic.
Atomic who?
Can I use your
bathroom? I have
atomic ache.

Atoms are made up of
three parts: electrons,
protons, and neutrons.

Q What do you call a **number** that can't **sit still?**

A A roamin' numeral.

Q How do **hurricanes** see?

A With one eye.

Q How does an astronomer cut his hair?

A Eclipse it.

Q Where does DNA swim?

A In the gene pool.

147

ATOM ANTICS

RESEARCHING CHEESE FOR MY SCIENCE PROJECT IS THE TASTIEST IDEA I'VE HAD ALL YEAR!

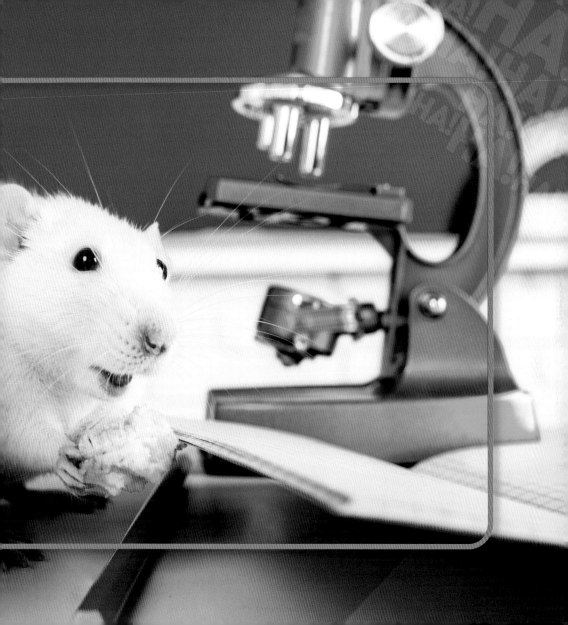

Q

Why did the star go to the bathroom?

A

It had to twinkle.

What does Q a spider bride wear?

A webbing dress. **A**

Q

What do you call a smart group of trees?

A brainforest.

A

EWAN: Do you like math jokes?
SAMARA: Sum of them.

KNOCK, KNOCK.

Who's there?
Value.
Value who?
Value be my valentine?

151

Q Why did the **atoms cross** the **road?**

A Because it was time to split.

Q What's the difference between **chemistry** and **cooking?**

A In chemistry, you should never lick the spoon.

154

There are eight planets in our solar system. They are Mercury, Venus, Earth, Mars, Jupiter, Saturn, Uranus, and Neptune.

KNOCK, KNOCK.

Who's there?
Planet.
Planet who?
I wanted to throw a party but had no time to planet.

155

Q

Why do microbiologists have so many social media followers?

A

Because their posts always go viral.

Q

What is a physicist's favorite snack?

A

Gram crackers.

KNOCK, KNOCK.

Who's there?
Plasma.
Plasma who?
Plasma sister stopped by? She said she was on her way over.

Plasma is a gas-like state of matter. Stars are mostly made of plasma.

159

Where do
Q
bacteria
go on vacation?

Germ-any.

Q Which is the **faster** runner: **hot** or **cold?**

A Hot, because you can catch a cold.

When bacteria picked up from the ground mixes with the sweat on a dog's paws, the chemical reaction creates a smell like corn chips!

Q Which season is the best for trampolining?

A Spring-time.

162

163

PHYSICIST 1:
Are you STILL lying
on the couch?
You're so lazy!

PHYSICIST 2:
I'm not lazy; I'm full
of potential energy.

HA!HA!

Q

What kind of TV does a biologist have?

A

A plasma screen.

Q

What did Obi-Wan Kenobi tell the geologist?

A

"May the quartz be with you."

A nanometer is a unit of measurement that is one billionth of a meter. A human hair is around 100,000 nanometers wide.

KNOCK, KNOCK.

Who's there?
Nano.
Nano who?
Nano your business, just open the door!

167

What do you call a **droid** that takes the **long way** around?

Q

Why did the oceanographer throw her books in the ocean?

A

To create a title wave.

Q

What is a **marine biologist's** favorite **game show?**

A

Whale of Fortune.

Q Why don't people tell bacteria jokes?

A Because they don't want to spread them around.

MOM ELECTRICAL CURRENT: I'm shocked at your behavior.

SON ELECTRICAL CURRENT: I'm sorry for how I conducted myself. I was amped up.

MOM ELECTRICAL CURRENT: You're grounded.

Q What do you call a **scientist** with a **chemistry book** in his **pocket?**

A Smarty-pants.

Q If H_2O is water, then what is H_2O_4?

A Drinking, of course!

KNOCK,
KNOCK.

Who's there?
Proton.
Proton who?
Proton your shoes,
and let's get
going!

A proton is an
electrically
charged particle
in the middle of
an atom.

173

174

Q Why did the botanist start a garden for her friends?

A She thought they would dig it.

Q Why did the **invisible man** flunk **science class?**

A Because the teacher always marked him absent.

TONGUE TWISTER!

Say this fast three times:

The shell shop sells shiny shells.

Q What is a leech's favorite fruit?

A A blood orange.

A robot dove was invented in ancient Greece in the year 350 B.C.E. by a mathematician named Archytas of Tarentum. It was powered by steam and could fly a short distance.

KNOCK, KNOCK.

Who's there?
Tech.
Tech who?
The science fair started. Let's go tech it out!

Why did the
T. rex **cross the road?**

Because the chicken didn't exist yet.

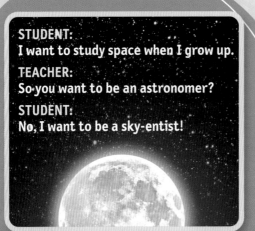

STUDENT:
I want to study space when I grow up.

TEACHER:
So you want to be an astronomer?

STUDENT:
No, I want to be a sky-entist!

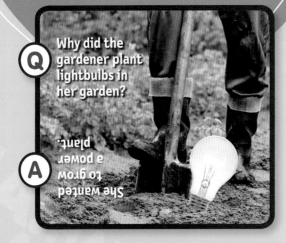

Q Why did the gardener plant lightbulbs in her garden?

A She wanted to grow a power plant.

Sir Isaac Newton was a scientist credited with discovering how gravity works in 1687.

KNOCK, KNOCK.
Who's there?
Newton.
Newton who?
Can you show me around? I'm Newton this school.

RESEARCH: Who's Copying Who?

Have you ever found yourself at a zoo imitating the apes? Betcha never thought your head scratches and "ooh-oohs" could count as scientific research! Apparently, mimicking chimps and apes can tell us something about how both humans and apes communicate.

Researchers from Sweden studied how humans and chimps interact at a zoo and found that we liked to imitate each other. Blow a chimp a kiss, and chances are a chimp will blow one back. If a chimp claps her hands, sometimes a human will clap theirs in return.

We like to think we are smarter than our closest ape relatives, but the study also revealed some of the smartest chimps could repeat every single gesture a human made at it. Researchers found that chimps are really good at copying—as good (or better) than a human toddler. So, the next time a chimp makes a funny face at you, she might just be copying the face you're making at her!

Chimpanzees communicate with each other with facial expressions and gestures as well as panting, drumming, and barking.

The study showed the chimps were aware they were being imitated and enjoyed it.

Mimicked actions included making funny faces, hand clapping, and kissing.

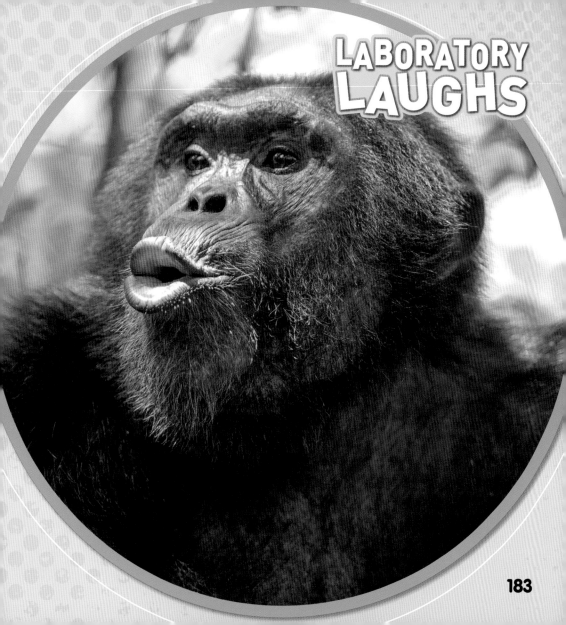

LABORATORY
LAUGHS

Q

Why did the science teacher write on the window?

A Because she wanted the lesson to be very clear.

TONGUE TWISTER!

Say this fast three times:

Sam sifts salty sand.

Q

Why did the giraffe fail science class?

A Because she had her head in the clouds.

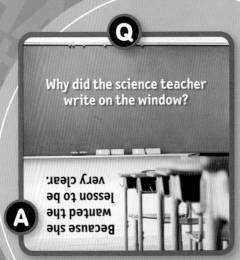
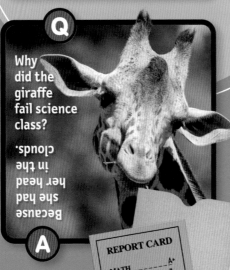

REPORT CARD

MATH _____ A+
ENGLISH _____ B
SCIENCE _____ A-
ART _____ C+
MUSIC _____ B+

Q

How are a **dog** and a **marine biologist** different?

A One wags a tail and the other tags a whale.

Genes are found inside the cells in our body. They carry the information that makes up our characteristics and traits, like eye color, hair color, and how tall we will be.

KNOCK, KNOCK.

Who's there?
Gene.
Gene who?
Who are you? I've never gene you here before.

Why are robots never afraid?

Because they have
nerves of steel.

A

187

Q Why did the scuba diver fail biology class?

A Because his grades were below C level.

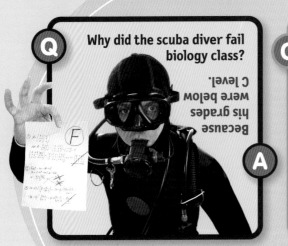

Q What do **baby mathematicians drink?**

A Formula.

Q What kind of notebook does a botanist use?

A A tree-ring binder.

METEOROLOGIST 1: Do you know what kind of music wind turbines like?

METEOROLOGIST 2: I heard they are huge metal fans.

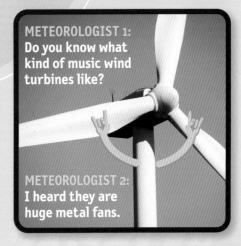

KNOCK, KNOCK.

Who's there?
Spore.
Spore who?
Are you spore you don't know who I am?

Spores are made by some plants in order to reproduce. They are picked up by the wind and land in different places where they grow into new plants.

Q Why did the bacteria fail their math test?

A They thought multiplication was the same as division.

PROFESSOR BUNSEN: What's the matter?

PROFESSOR BEAKER: I think I lost an electron.

PROFESSOR BUNSEN: Yes, you really have to keep an ion them.

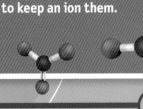

Q If fruit comes from a fruit tree, where do chickens come from?

A Poul-trees.

Q What is a botanist's favorite month?

A Sep-timber.

KNOCK, KNOCK.
Who's there?
Algae.
Algae who?
I stopped by to drop off your algae-bra homework.

Algae are plantlike organisms that make oxygen. They grow in water, on trees, and even on some animals like sloths or turtles.

193

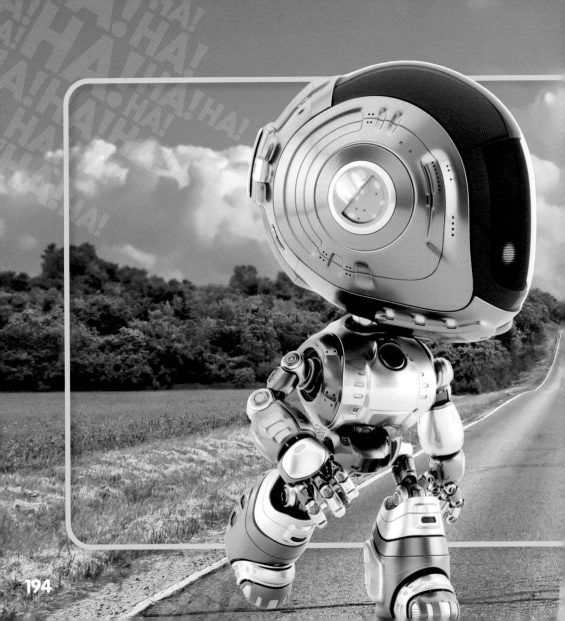

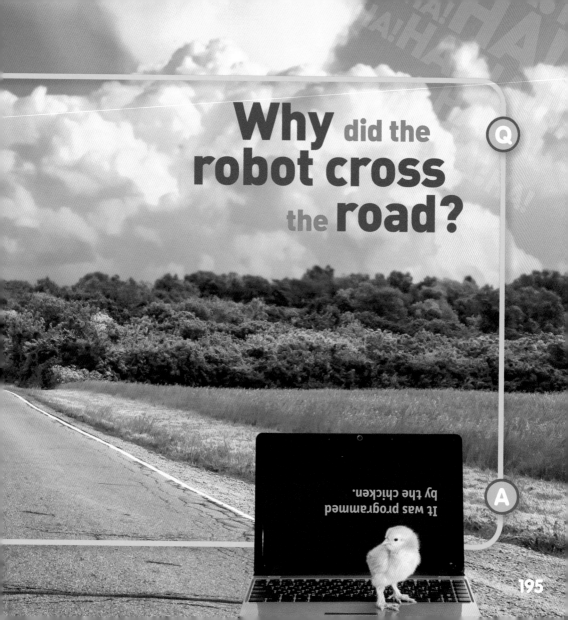

Why did the robot cross the road?

Q

It was programmed by the chicken.

A

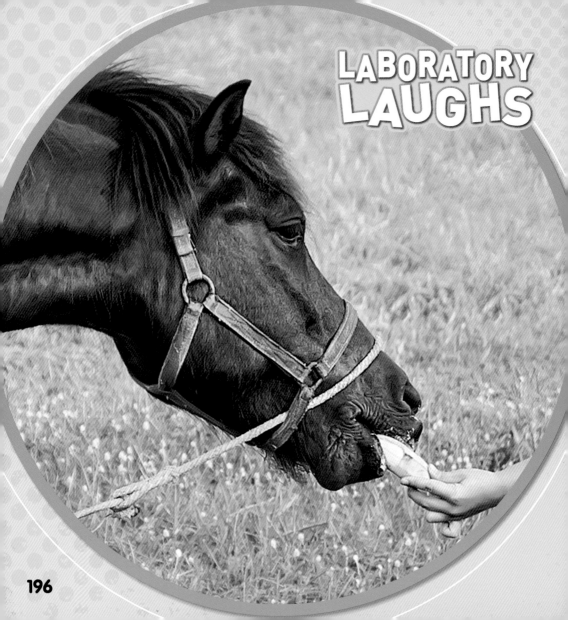

LABORATORY
LAUGHS

RESEARCH: Mind Your Stable Manners!

We know a lot about horses. We know they are found in almost every country in the world and that they have been domesticated for more than 5,000 years. We know they can sleep both lying down and standing up, and we know that there are around 60 million of them on the planet. That's a lot of horse facts! But until a few years ago, we had no idea what their favorite flavor is!

In a scientific study you had no idea was happening, Dr. Deborah Goodwin from the United Kingdom determined that horses would prefer a banana over a carrot any day. Who knew? Throwing an all-equine dinner party? Make sure you serve fenugreek (an herb used commonly in curries) to keep your brunching broncos happy.

Not only was the good doctor able to rank horses' top eight flavor preferences, she was able to figure out the three flavors they will turn their noses up at. Whew! Avoid nutmeg and coriander to keep your picky ponies pigging out.

Horses' top-ranked flavors are:
1. Fenugreek, 2. Banana, 3. Artificial cherry flavor, 4. Rosemary, 5. Cumin, 6. Carrot, 7. Peppermint, 8. Oregano.

Manufacturers of horse medication and supplements can use this information to produce products that horses will take more easily.

While cherry came third on the list, real cherries are toxic to horses. Only artificial cherry flavor should be used.

Q

What do you get if you cross a pirate and a droid?

A Aaarr2-D2.

Q

What kind of flowers do bacteria like?

A Germ-aniums.

Telescopes are mostly used to see planets and stars. They were invented in 1608.

199

Q

How do archaeologists address letters?

Tomb it may concern ...

A

AIR MAIL

Now **that** was funny!

JOKEFINDER

ILLUSTRATION CREDITS

Since 1888, the National Geographic Society has funded more than 14,000 research, conservation, education, and storytelling projects around the world. National Geographic Partners distributes a portion of the funds it receives from your purchase to National Geographic Society to support programs including the conservation of animals and their habitats. To learn more, visit natgeo.com/info.

For more information, visit nationalgeographic .com, call 1-877-873-6846, or write to the following address:

National Geographic Partners, LLC
1145 17th Street N.W.
Washington, DC 20036-4688 U.S.A.

For librarians and teachers: nationalgeographic .com/books/librarians-and-educators

More for kids from National Geographic: natgeokids.com

National Geographic Kids magazine inspires children to explore their world with fun yet educational articles on animals, science, nature, and more. Using fresh storytelling and amazing photography, *Nat Geo Kids* shows kids ages 6 to 14 the fascinating truth about the world—and why they should care. **natgeo.com/subscribe**

For rights or permissions inquiries, please contact National Geographic Books Subsidiary Rights: bookrights@natgeo.com

Art directed by Sanjida Rashid
Editorial, Design, and Production by Plan B Book Packagers

Trade paperback ISBN: 978-1-4263-7151-6
Reinforced library binding ISBN:
978-1-4263-7152-3

Printed in China
21/PPS/1